#1 THE CHALLENGE OF SAMUKAI!

GREG FARSHTEY • Writer
PAULO HENRIQUE • Artist
LAURIE E. SMITH • Colorist

New York

LEGO® NINJAGO Masters of Spinjitzu
#1 "The Challenge of Samukai!"
Production by SHELLY STERNER, Nelson Design Group, LLC
Associate Editor – MICHAEL PETRANEK
JIM SALICRUP
Editor-in-Chief

ISBN: 978-1-59707-297-7 paperback edition
ISBN: 978-1-59707-298-4 hardcover edition

Printed in the US
March 2012 by Lifetouch Printing
5126 Forest Hills Ct.
Loves Park, IL 61111

Distributed by Macmillan

MEET THE MASTERS
OF SPINJITZU...
JAY

COLE

ZANE

KAI

NYA

LEGO NINJAGO

Masters of Spinjitzu

The four-armed gentleman's name is Samukai. He is the ruler of the Underworld. At least, that is the title he has.
Since the arrival of Lord Garmadon in his realm, though, Samukai has begun to wonder if he is the master here, or just another slave.

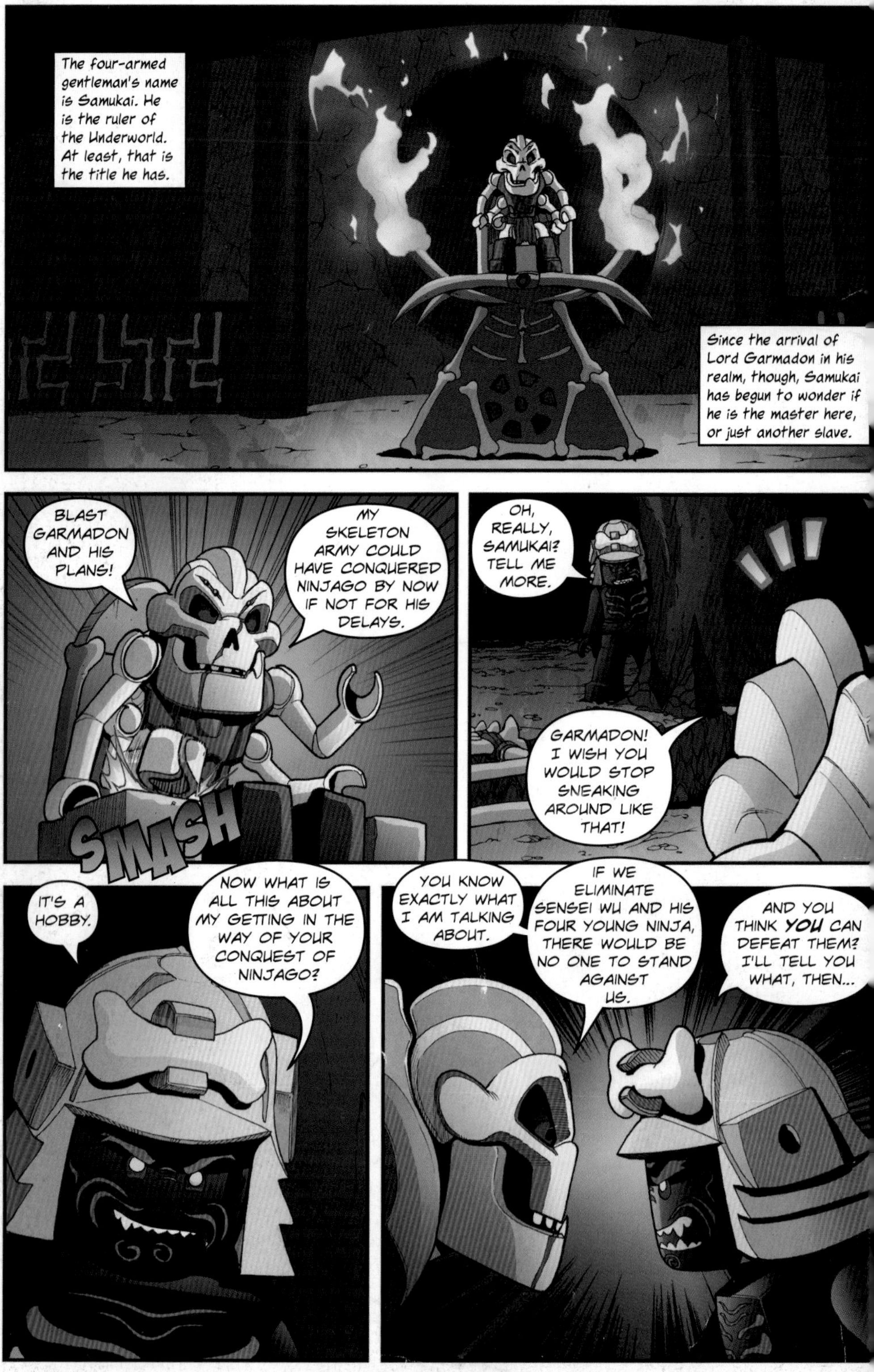

BLAST GARMADON AND HIS PLANS!

MY SKELETON ARMY COULD HAVE CONQUERED NINJAGO BY NOW IF NOT FOR HIS DELAYS.

SMASH

OH, REALLY, SAMUKAI? TELL ME MORE.

GARMADON! I WISH YOU WOULD STOP SNEAKING AROUND LIKE THAT!

IT'S A HOBBY.

NOW WHAT IS ALL THIS ABOUT MY GETTING IN THE WAY OF YOUR CONQUEST OF NINJAGO?

YOU KNOW EXACTLY WHAT I AM TALKING ABOUT.

IF WE ELIMINATE SENSEI WU AND HIS FOUR YOUNG NINJA, THERE WOULD BE NO ONE TO STAND AGAINST US.

AND YOU THINK **YOU** CAN DEFEAT THEM? I'LL TELL YOU WHAT, THEN...

LET'S MAKE A BET.
THE WAGER, PART ONE
GREG FARSHTEY -- HONORABLE WRITER
PAULO HENRIQUE -- AUGUST ARTIST
LAURIE E. SMITH -- HUMBLE COLORIST
BRYAN SENKA -- LOYAL LETTERER
MICHAEL PETRANEK -- EDITORIAL STUDENT
JIM SALICRUP -- EDITORIAL MASTER

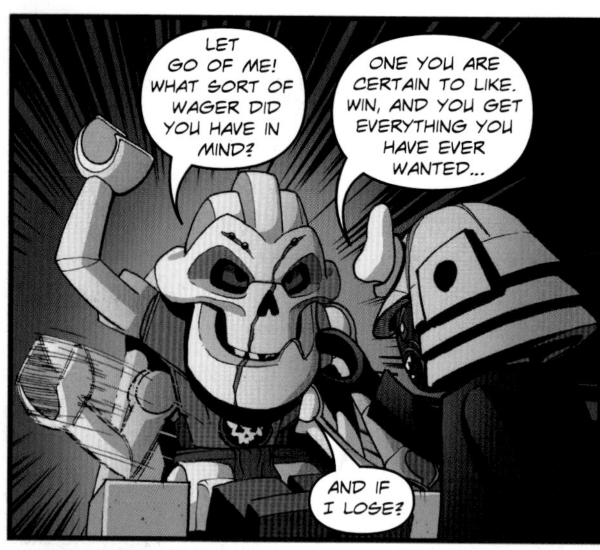
LET GO OF ME! WHAT SORT OF WAGER DID YOU HAVE IN MIND?
ONE YOU ARE CERTAIN TO LIKE. WIN, AND YOU GET EVERYTHING YOU HAVE EVER WANTED...
AND IF I LOSE?

SURELY YOU DON'T ADMIT TO THAT POSSIBILITY?
AH, BUT YOU DID L ONCE BEF DIDN'T Y

"YOU KNOW THAT WHEN I WAS FIRST EXILED HERE, SO LONG AGO," SAYS GARMADON...
"YOU WANTED ME TO BE ONE MORE OF YOUR SOLDIERS. I SAID NO, AND WE FOUGHT TO SETTLE MATTERS."

"ALL THOSE ARMS, AND YOU STILL COULDN'T LAY A HAND ON ME. AND THAT IS HOW WE BECAME... ALLIES."

I STILL THINK YOU CHEATED. BUT WHAT ARE THE TERMS OF THIS BET?

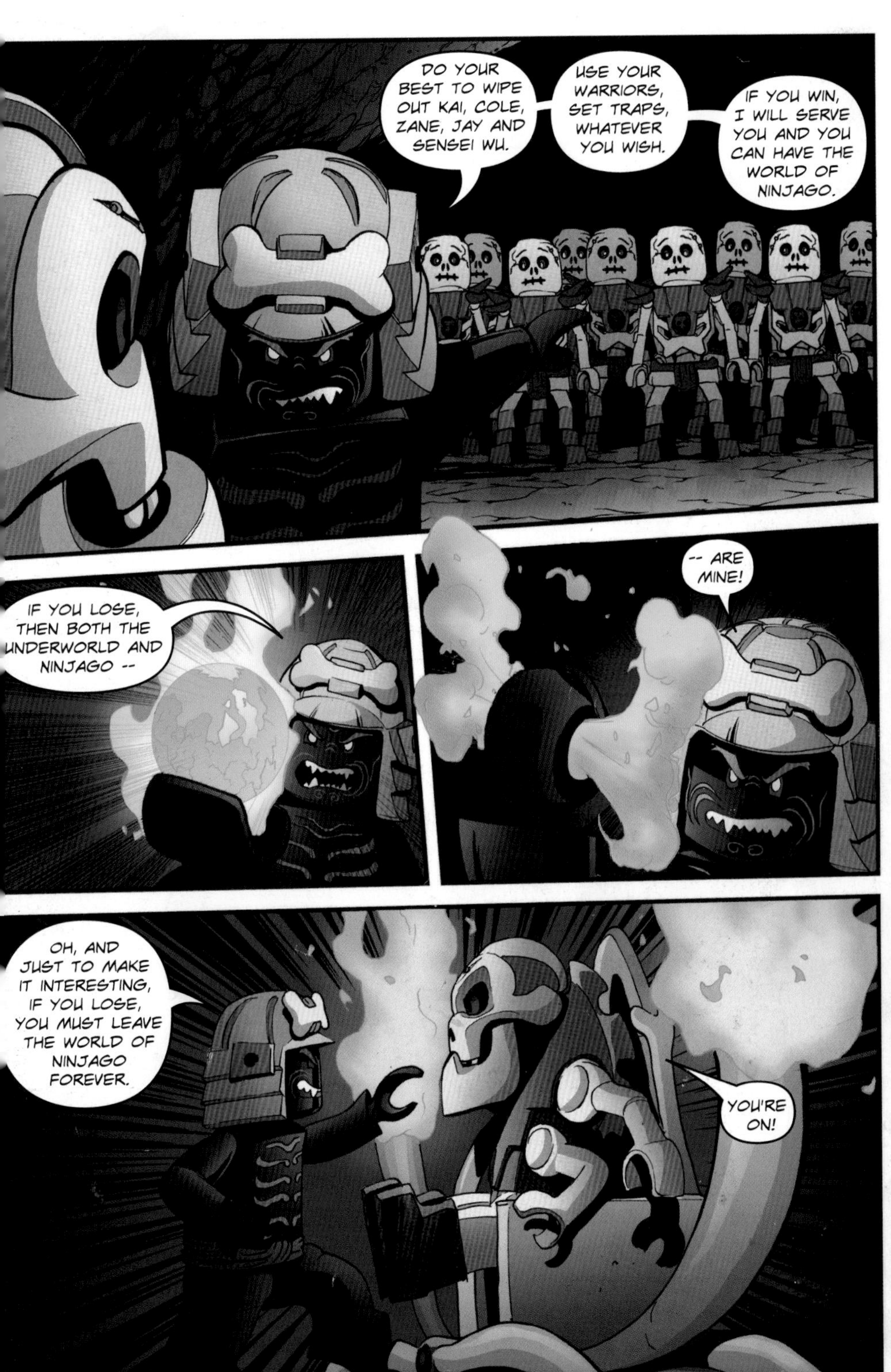
DO YOUR BEST TO WIPE OUT KAI, COLE, ZANE, JAY AND SENSEI WU.
USE YOUR WARRIORS, SET TRAPS, WHATEVER YOU WISH.
IF YOU WIN, I WILL SERVE YOU AND YOU CAN HAVE THE WORLD OF NINJAGO.
IF YOU LOSE, THEN BOTH THE UNDERWORLD AND NINJAGO --
-- ARE MINE!
OH, AND JUST TO MAKE IT INTERESTING, IF YOU LOSE, YOU MUST LEAVE THE WORLD OF NINJAGO FOREVER.
YOU'RE ON!

GARMADON IS A FOOL. HE THINKS I DON'T KNOW THERE IS MORE TO THIS WAGER THAN WHAT HE HAS SAID.

BUT I WILL DEFEAT THE SENSEI AND HIS TEAM OF CHILDREN, AND THEN GARMADON AS WELL.

THIS WAGER IS AS GOOD AS WON.

Laurie "Let-it-ride" E. Smith — Colorist • Bettin' Bryan Senka — Letterer
Michael "The Player" Petranek — Associate Editor • Jim "Jackpot" Salicrup — Editor-in-Chief
TO WIN MY WAGER WITH GARMADON, I MUST DESTROY THESE FOUR NINJA.
AND TO DO THAT, I NEED KNOWLEDGE... I MUST KNOW ALL I CAN OF HOW SENSEI WU'S TEAM CAME TO BE.
"IT TRULY BEGAN," SAYS SAMUKAI, "MANY, MANY THOUSANDS OF YEARS AGO, WHEN THE FATHER OF SENSEI WU AND GARMADON CREATED FOUR GOLDEN WEAPONS.
"SEPARATELY, THESE WEAPONS WERE INCREDIBLY POWERFUL. TOGETHER, THEIR MIGHT WOULD BE DEVASTATING.
"UPON THEIR FATHER'S DEATH, THE WEAPONS WERE ENTRUSTED TO THE CARE OF WU AND GARMADON.
BUT GARMADON DESIRED THE WEAPONS FOR HIMSELF, AND A BATTLE ERUPTED.

"THE FUTURE SENSEI WU WAS THE VICTOR, AND GARMADON WAS BANISHED TO THE UNDERWORLD... MY REALM. IT SEEMED THAT THE GOLDEN WEAPONS WERE SAFE FOREVER.

"SENSEI WU HID THE WEAPONS AWAY. USING THE POWER OF SPINJITZU, HE FOUGHT FOR 'JUSTICE' THROUGHOUT THE LAND AND BECAME A HERO TO THOSE IDIOTIC MORTALS ON THE WORLD OF NINJAGO.

"STILL, HE NEVER RELAXED HIS GUARD. HE KNEW THE FOUR WEAPONS OF SPINJITZU HAD TO BE PROTECTED. AND ONE DAY, AS HE REACHED OUT ACROSS THE PLANET WITH HIS SENSES, HE SUDDENLY KNEW...

"GARMADON HAD RETURNED!

"THE SENSEI'S EVIL BROTHER HAD ALLIED WITH ME AND PLANNED TO USE MY SKELETON ARMY TO STEAL THE FOUR WEAPONS AND CONQUER NINJAGO. THE INVASION HAD ALREADY BEGUN!

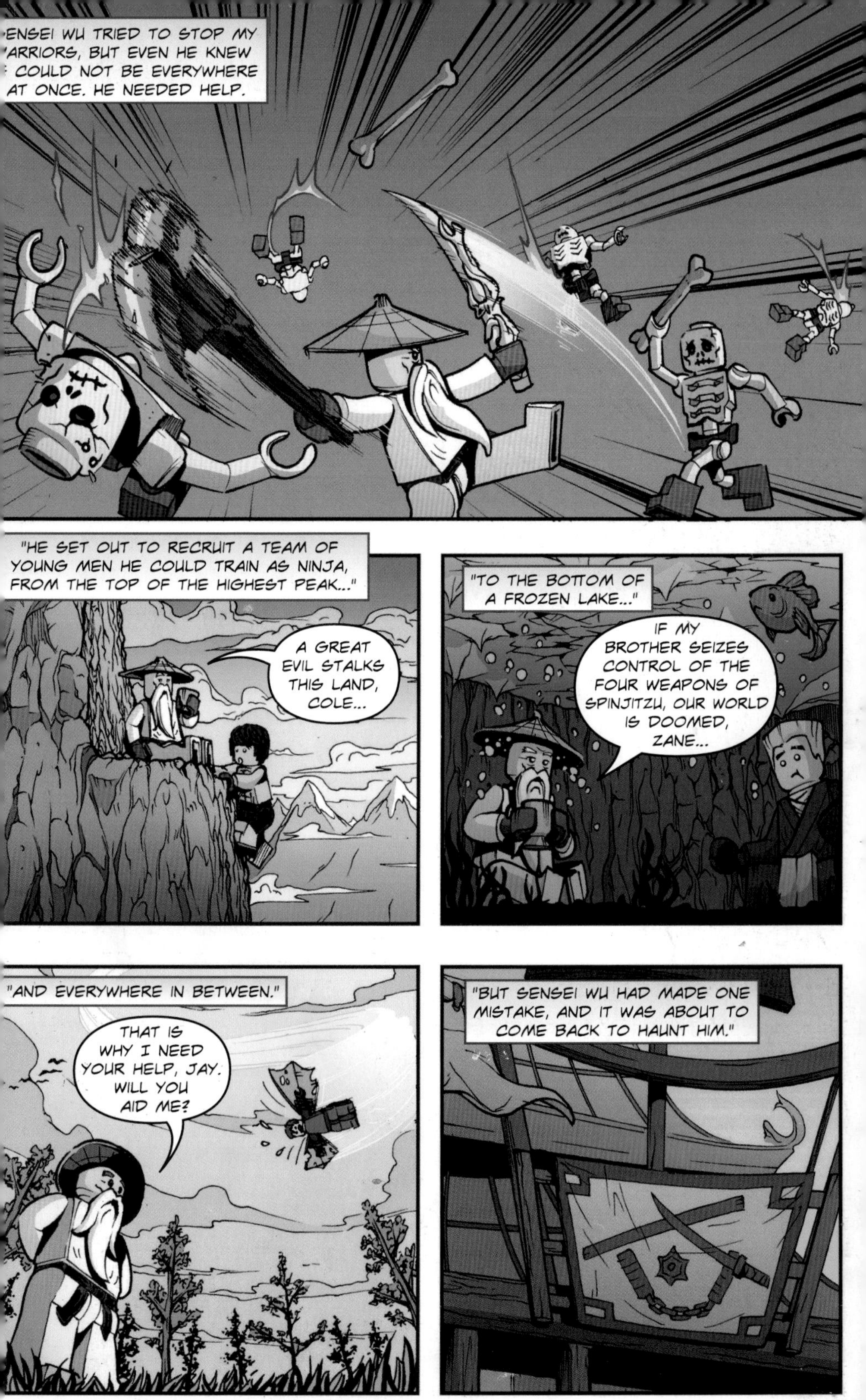

ENSEI WU TRIED TO STOP MY
ARRIORS, BUT EVEN HE KNEW
COULD NOT BE EVERYWHERE
AT ONCE. HE NEEDED HELP.

"HE SET OUT TO RECRUIT A TEAM OF YOUNG MEN HE COULD TRAIN AS NINJA, FROM THE TOP OF THE HIGHEST PEAK..."
A GREAT EVIL STALKS THIS LAND, COLE...

"TO THE BOTTOM OF A FROZEN LAKE..."
IF MY BROTHER SEIZES CONTROL OF THE FOUR WEAPONS OF SPINJITZU, OUR WORLD IS DOOMED, ZANE...

"AND EVERYWHERE IN BETWEEN."
THAT IS WHY I NEED YOUR HELP, JAY. WILL YOU AID ME?

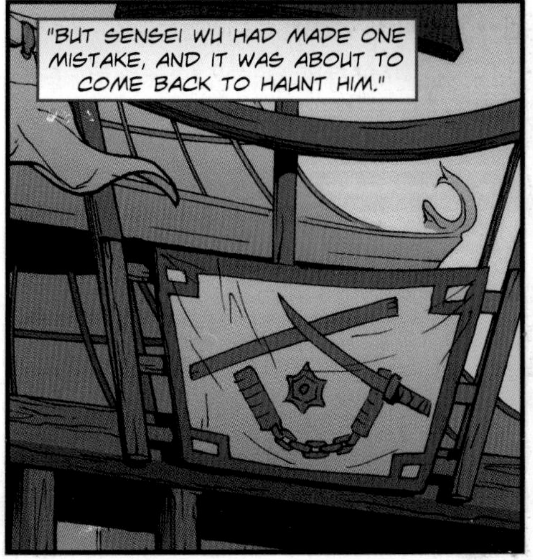

"BUT SENSEI WU HAD MADE ONE MISTAKE, AND IT WAS ABOUT TO COME BACK TO HAUNT HIM."

WHAT DO YOU THINK? IT'S A SWORD.
SOMEDAY, A MIGHTY WARRIOR WILL CARRY THIS INTO BATTLE--
AND IF HE LIVES, HE'LL COME BACK AND USE IT ON YOU.
HELP! RUN! THEY'RE EVERY-WHERE!
WHAT IS GOIN ON OUT THERE
OH, MY-- SKELETONS WARRIORS! THE VILLAGE IS IN DANGER!
I'LL SHOW THEM THEY CAN'T GO AROUND ATTACKING INNOCENT PEOPLE!
KAI, ARE YOU CRAZY? YOU COULD GET HURT!

"BUT KAI WASN'T HARMED. IN FACT, HE FOUGHT WELL. BUT WHILE HE WAS BATTLING SOME OF MY WARRIORS--
"THE OTHERS WERE TAKING WHAT WE HAD REALLY COME THERE FOR: KAI'S SISTER AND A LITTLE SOMETHING THAT WAS, UNKNOWN TO THEM, CONCEALED INSIDE THE BANNER OF THEIR SHOP."
HELP! KAI!
RIPPPPP
"IT WAS ONLY LATER THAT ENSEI WU WOULD ELL KAI JUST WHY 'E HAD ATTACKED THAT LITTLE VILLAGE."
LONG AGO, I ASKED YOUR FATHER TO MAKE A MAP FOR ME, SHOWING WHERE THE FOUR WEAPONS OF SPINJITZU WERE HIDDEN.
THAT MAP WAS CONCEALED IN THE 4WEAPONS BANNER-- AND NOW GARMADON AND HIS SKELETON ALLIES HAVE IT.
I DON'T CARE ABOUT ANY OF THAT. I WANT MY SISTER BACK!
ARE YOU GOING TO HELP ME FIND HER, OR DO I DO IT ON MY OWN?
TO SAVE YOUR SISTER, YOU NEED TRAINING.
JOIN MY TEAM-- BECOME A NINJA-- AND TOGETHER, WE WILL STOP GARMADON AND SAVE NYA.

ALL RIGHT, YOU ASKED FOR IT.

HAI!

HUH? WHERE DID YOU GO?

I AM HERE. WHERE ELSE SHOULD I BE?

OR DO YOU EXPECT YOUR OPPONENTS TO POLITELY STAN STILL AND WAIT FOR YOU TO HIT THEM?

OWWW

TRY THIS ON FOR SIZE, I'LL-- HEY! NO ONE MOVES THAT FAST!

WHAT A SILLY THING TO SAY. OBVIOUSLY, I DO.

AND THAT IS NOT ALL I DO. BEHOLD, KAI, THE POWER OF SPINJITZU!
WOW!
HOW DO YOU DO THAT? TEACH IT TO ME, PLEASE.
SPINJITZU CAN BE LEARNED, BUT IT CANNOT BE TAUGHT. YOU WILL KNOW ALL THERE IS TO KNOW, IN TIME.
TIME! EVERYTHING TAKES TIME-- BUT NYA MAY NOT HAVE MUCH TIME LEFT.
GARMADON ORDERED HER TAKEN FOR A REASON. SHE WILL NOT BE HARMED... YET.
RUSHING TO HER RESCUE WILL ONLY GIVE MY BROTHER TWO CAPTIVES, INSTEAD OF ONE.

"SO KAI WORKED...
"HARDER TH
HE EVER HA
IN HIS LIFE.
"AND WORKED...
"PREPARING FO
THE DAY HE WO
BATTLE GARMAD
AND MYSELF.

"KAI'S FINAL TEST WAS TO BATTLE JAY, COLE, AND ZANE, SENSEI WU'S THREE NINJA.
"TO FAIL AGAINST THESE THREE WOULD ROB KAI OF ANY CHANCE OF RESCUING HIS SISTER.
"BUT HE DID NOT FAIL. NOW HE FIGHTS ALONGSIDE THE OTHER THREE, WHO HAVE BECOME HIS BEST FRIENDS. TOGETHER, THEY DARE TO TTEMPT TO STOP GARMADON'S MASTER PLAN."

THEY SHALL NOT SUCCEED. THEY MAY WIN BATTLES, BUT ONLY SAMUKAI CAN WIN THE WAR.

I SHALL BEGIN WITH KAI. HE HOLDS HIS NEW FRIENDS DEAR TO HIS HEART...
IMAGINE HOW HE WOULD FEE IF THEY TRIED HURT HIM.

I KNOW JUST HOW TO MAKE THAT HAPPEN.
BEFORE NINJAGO'S SUN HAS RISEN AND SET ONCE MORE, I WILL STRIKE...

AND THE FIRST OF THE NINJA SHALL FALL!

ot far from the temporary campsite
f Sensei Wu and his four ninja...
OKAY, SO, WHEN I SEE KAI, I CHASE AFTER HIM.
NO, NUCKAL, YOU LET HIM CHASE AFTER YOU.

RIGHT, GENERAL KRUNCHA, BUT NO MATTER WHAT, DON'T LET HIM NEAR THE CRYSTAL CAVES.
NO, YOU NUMBSKULL, YOU WANT HIM TO GO INTO THE CRYSTAL CAVES! YOU'RE SUPPOSED TO LEAD HIM THERE!

HOW I'M SUPPOSED TO TRAP A NINJA WITH HELP LIKE THIS, I DON'T--

WHACK
YOU WERE WRONG, GENERAL. MY SKULL'S NOT NUMB. I SURE FELT THAT!

TURN ABOUT
"GORILLA" GREG FARSHTEY -- WRITER
"PILEDRIVER" PAULO HENRIQUE -- ARTIST
"LOCK 'N' LOAD" LAURIE E. SMITH -- COLORIST
"BAD BOY" BRYAN SENKA -- LETTERER
"MAD DOG" MICHAEL PETRANEK -- ASSOCIATE EDITOR
"JAWBREAKER" JIM SALICRUP -- EDITOR-IN-CHIEF
I'M SO DONE... AGAIN. ALL RIGHT, NUCKAL, LET'S GO OVER IT ONE MORE TIME.

THERE HE IS! NOW TRY TO REMEMBER WHAT YOU'RE SUPPOSED TO DO, PLEASE?
NO WORRIES, BOSS.
HA HA! HEY, SKELETON OVER HERE!
WHAT THE--?
COME BACK HERE!
CAN'T CATCH ME! ALL THAT MUSCLE SLOWS YOU DOWN.
THAT'S WHERE I'M NOT SUPPOSED TO GO... NO, THAT'S WHERE I AM SUPPOSED TO GO. THAT'S WHERE SAMUKAI SET THE TRAP.
THE CRYSTAL CAVES? SENSEI WU SAID TO STAY OUT OF THERE, BUT I'M NOT LETTING THAT SKELETON GET AWAY.

HEE HEE! KRUNCHA LL BE PROUD OF ME-- KNOCKING ON UCKAL'S HEAD TODAY.
WAIT UNTIL I CATCH UP TO YOU. THEN YOU'LL SEE SOME HEAD-KNOCKING YOU WON'T FORGET.
WHEW! WHAT'S WRONG WITH ME? I DON'T FEEL SO GOOD...
NUCKAL'S OTTEN AWAY... E COULD BE ANYWHERE IN HERE.
I BETTER GO TELL THE SENSEI.
STILL FEEL WEIRD. I WONDER IF I'VE BEEN TRAINING TOO HARD?
WELL, THE SENSEI WILL KNOW WHAT'S THE MATTER.
HEY, GUYS, I'M BACK.

LOOK WHO JUST WALKED RIGHT INTO OUR CAMP!
WELL, HE WON'T BE WALKING OUT AGAIN.
ENOUGH TALK-- LET'S GET HIM.
WHAT? HOLD ON, IT'S ME! IT'S KAI!

SENSEI WU, TELL THEM I'M ME. HAT'S GOING N AROUND HERE?
YOU WON'T FOOL US WITH SO OBVIOUS A TRICK. DEFEAT HIM, MY NINJA!
I DON'T KNOW WHAT'S HAPPENING, BUT THIS ISN'T A HEALTHY PLACE TO BE RIGHT NOW!
STOP HIM! DON'T LET HIM GET AWAY!
HIS WILL LOW HIM DOWN.
SORRY, ZANE, I TAUGHT YOU THAT MOVE, REMEMBER?
I'LL HEAD FOR THE RIVER. MAYBE I CAN HIDE UNDERWATER.
BUT WHAT'S GOTTEN INTO THEM? COULD IT BE THEY AREN'T REALLY WHO THEY SEEM TO BE?
YIIIIIIIII!

WHAT--?? HOW--?? I'M ME, BUT--

I LOOK LIKE A SKELETON! NO WONDER THE OTHERS WERE CHASING ME!

HOW CAN I CONVINCE THEM I'M ME? BETTER YET, HOW DO I KEEP THEM FROM POUNDING ME INTO THE GROUND?

HE MUST HAVE CROSSED THE RIVER SOMEWHERE. SPLIT UP! FIND HIM!

YOU DO THAT, GUYS. I AM GOING TO HEAD BACK TO MY VILLAGE. SOMEBODY THERE WILL BE ABLE TO TELL WHO I REALLY AM.

ai arrives in his village like this...
HI, EVERYONE! IT'S KAI-- REALLY, IT IS.

But what the villagers see is this...

o, is it any wonder that they react like this?
SKELETON! GET OUT OF OUR VILLAGE!
GO BACK TO WHERE YOU BELONG!
OW! HEY! STOP IT!

Driven from the village, Kai wonders what to do next.
NOW WHAT?
I... WAIT A MINUTE. SOMETHING THAT VILLAGER SAID, ABOUT GOING BACK WHERE I BELONG. WHERE DID ALL THIS START?

THE CRYSTAL CAVE!

MAYBE THE ANSWER IS THERE. IT'S WORTH A TRY.
HEY! THERE HE IS!

OH, NOT NOW...
AFTER HIM!
For the rest of the day, Kai fights...
KA-TANG
And flees, trying to get back to the Crystal Cave.
SPROING
I LOST THEM, FOR NOW. BUT THIS PROVES I'M RIGHT--
WHY POST A GUARD UNLESS THE CAVE IS IMPORTANT SOMEHOW?
A LITTLE SPINJITZU WILL TAKE CARE OF YOU, BONES.
HEY, WHAT ARE YOU- STOP! HELP!
WHOO! THE WHOLE WORLD IS SPINNING ROUND AND ROUND AND ROUND...

HE'S HEADED INTO THE CAVE.
THEN HE'S TRAPPED HIMSELF AT LAST.
SO, WHAT ARE WE WAITING FOR?
LET'S GET HIM!
WOW, I'M FEELING WEIRD AGAIN... IT'S WORSE THIS TIME...
AND THE GUYS ARE STILL AFTER ME. IF THEY CATCH ME NOW, I'M THROUGH!
UP THERE-- IT LOOKS LIKE ANOTHER WAY OUT.
LET'S HOPE RUNNING THROUGH THE CAVE A SECOND TIME UNDID WHAT HAPPENED, BECAUSE I CAN'T RUN ANYMORE.
MADE IT! BUT HOW WILL I KNOW IF IT WORKED?

HEY, IT'S KAI.
WHAT IS HE DOING HERE?
KAI, DID YOU SEE A SKELETON WARRIOR COME OUT THIS WAY?

IT'S A FUNNY STORY, GUYS, AND... **OH, NO!**

WHAT'S THE MATTER, KAI?
HEY, DON'T YOU RECOGNIZE US? WE'RE YOUR BUDDIES.
WHY ARE YOU LOOKING AT US THAT WAY?

WELL, I'LL TELL YOU... BUT I'M NOT SURE YOU'RE GOING TO BELIEVE IT.
End.

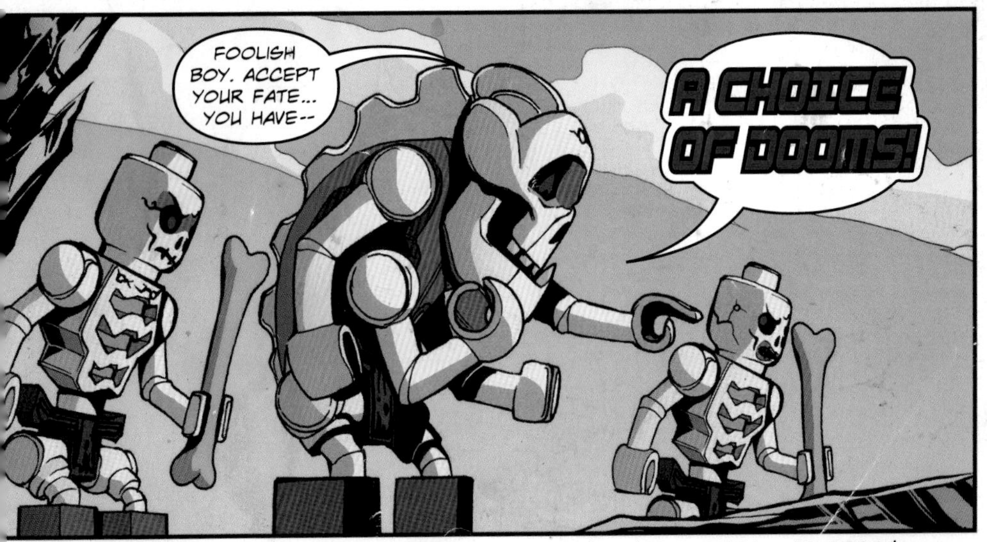

GREG FARSHTEY -- WRITER * PAULO HENRIQUE -- ARTIST * LAURIE E. SMITH -- COLORIST *
'AN SENKA -- LETTERER * MICHAEL PETRANEK -- ASSOCIATE EDITOR * JIM SALICRUP -- EDITOR-IN-CHIEF

SOME CHOICE... BEHIND ONE DOOR, A MONSTER WOLF WHO PROBABLY THINKS OF NINJA AS DESSERT...

AND BEHIND THE OTHER, 100 AXES, ALL READY TO TURN ME INTO BITS AND PIECES.

WHICH ONE DO I CHOOSE? YOU WOULD THINK I'D HAVE HAD ENOUGH PRACTICE MAKING CHOICES IN THE LAST DAY...

Yesterday.

AS LEADER OF THE NINJA, COLE, YOU MUST BE ABLE TO MAKE HARD DECISIONS QUICKLY.

THAT IS WHY I HAVE DEVISED THIS TEST.

I UNDERSTAN SENSEI. I AM FOLLOW THE NORT PATH, AND THEN THE SCROLL AND THE FIRST LINE I COME TO A FORK.

OKAY, LET'S SEE. "BANDITS HAVE STOLEN A FORTUNE IN TREASURE AND HAVE ESCAPED OVER ONE OF THESE TWO PATHS. CHOOSE THE ONE YOU BELIEVE THEY HAVE TAKEN."

HMMM.
THE PATH INTO THE FOREST WOULD BE A LOT EASIER, AND THERE ARE PLENTY OF TRACKS IN THE MUD HERE. BUT THEY AREN'T VERY DEEP.

THE TREASURE MUST BE GOLD OR JEWELS, AND SO IT WOULD BE HEAVY.
THE TRACKS ON THIS PATH ARE MUCH DEEPER, SO THEY MUST HAVE GONE THIS WAY.

ater...
WHEW!
I'VE BEEN WALKING THIS PATH FOR HOURS AND NOTHING. WAIT, WHAT'S THAT?

IT'S FROM THE SENSEI. "YOU CHOSE THE WRONG PATH. A TREASURE NEED NOT BE HEAVY TO BE VALUABLE. THE BANDITS STOLE A BOOK OF KNOWLEDGE. TRAVEL TO THE OTHER SIDE OF THE HILL."
OKAY, THEN I'LL DO BETTER NEXT TIME.

ter...
A LONG DROP... AND ANOTHER NOTE.

"THE BANDITS HAVE CROSSED THE RIVER, AND SO MUST YOU. WILL YOU GO DOWN OR ACROSS?"

IT WILL TAKE TOO LONG TO CLIMB DOWN, CROSS THE RIVER, AND CLIMB BACK UP.
BUT IF I TRY TO SWING ACROSS, THAT DRAGON HAWK WILL GET ME. UNLESS...
SKREEEK!
MAYBE I CAN HITCH A RIDE!
WHOA! KAI WOULD HAVE LOVED THIS!
SKREEKK!
OKAY, I SHOULD HAVE THOUGHT ABOUT GETTING BACK DOWN. WELL, I CAN ALWAYS--
--LET GO!

FORTUNATELY, WHEN YOU KNOW SPINJITZU, FALLING ISN'T SO SCARY.
MY TURNADO SLOWS MY FALL AND HERE I AM, ACROSS THE RIVER. WONDER WHAT SURPRISE WAITS FOR ME HERE?
OH. THAT SURPRISE.
What Cole could not know, as he met his new challenge, was that Samukai's spies had informed him of all that was taking place.
SO, THE YOUNG NINJA HAS TO MAKE CHOICES? THEN LET'S GIVE HIM ONE.
Samukai arranged an ambush, capturing Kai and Jay as bait for a trap for Cole.

Meanwhile, unaware of what has happened to his friends...

WHEN SENSEI WU ARRANGES A TEST, HE DOESN'T MESS AROUND!

BUT HE'S GOING TO HAVE TO FIND BETTER FIGHTER IF HE WANTS TO DO MORE THAN SLOW ME DOWN.

ON TO THE NEXT CHALLENGE-- AND THERE'S THE NOTE.

I'LL TAKE THAT!

SAMUKAI!

HOW NICE. YOU REMEMBER. I HAVE A TEST OF MY OWN FOR YOU.

I HAVE TRAPPED KAI AND JAY AND ONLY YOU CAN SAVE THEM.

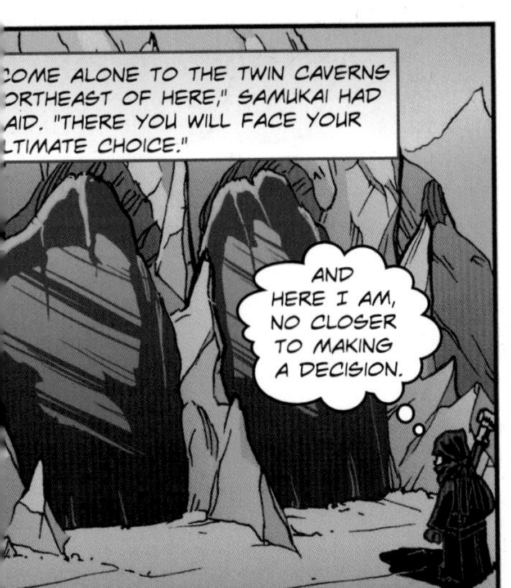

COME ALONE TO THE TWIN CAVERNS ORTHEAST OF HERE," SAMUKAI HAD AID. "THERE YOU WILL FACE YOUR LTIMATE CHOICE."
AND HERE I AM, NO CLOSER TO MAKING A DECISION.

COULD ONE OF THESE TRAPS BE AN ILLUSION? THEY BOTH LOOK REAL ENOUGH.

CHOOSE, NINJA! NOW!

THAT WOLF HAS TO BE REAL, DOWN TO THE FANGS AND CLAWS.
DON'T PUSH ME!

AND THOSE AXES LOOK PLENTY SHARP. THOSE FLIES HAD BETTER BE CAREFUL THEY DON'T GET SLICED, AND...

FLIES?
WAIT A MINUTE...
OF COURSE!

I CHOOSE
THIS ONE,
SAMUKAI!
KRASSSHHH

HA! EITHER
I'VE BECOME
SUPER-STRONG,
OR YOU NEED
A BETTER
AXE-MAKER.

HOW?
HOW DID
YOU GUESS
THE RIGHT
DOOR?
IT WAS THE FLIES.
WHEN I SAW THEM
BUZZING AROUND THE
BLADES, I KNEW THE
AXES WEREN'T METAL--
THEY WERE MADE
OF SUGAR. SO THIS
HAD TO BE THE
SAFE DOOR.

THERE IS NO SAFETY FOR YOU! GET HIM!
DID I FORGET TO MENTION I PICKED UP SOME SPARE DAGGERS FROM SENSEI WU'S FIGHTERS?
OH, AND I SPOTTED JAY AND KAI BACK IN THE SHADOWS, TOO--
DOES HIS MEAN 'RE INVITED TO THE PARTY?
I'D SAY SO!
gainst the power of three ninja, two skeleton warriors and little chance. Even 20 warriors might fall!
GREAT WORK-OUT!
YEAH, MY MUSCLES WERE GETTING STIFF WITH ALL THOSE ROPES.
YOU GUYS FINISH THESE TWO OFF. SAMUKAI IS MINE!

I THINK NOT.
I HAVE NOTHING TO GAIN FROM BATTLING YOU. BUT WE WILL SEE EACH OTHER AGAIN SOON.
SOONER THAN YOU THINK, YOU--! GONE!
DON'T WORRY ABOUT IT, COLE. HE'LL TURN UP AGAIN.
MAYBE I DON'T FEEL LIKE WAITING. COME ON, LET'S HEAD BACK TO CAMP. WE HAVE PLANS TO MAKE.
SOUNDS LIKE MORE ACTION ON THE WAY. WE'VE GOT TO STAY BATTLE-READY.
ONLY ONE THING BOTHERS ME-- I DIDN'T GET TO FINISH SENSEI WU'S TEST.
YOU KNOW SOMETHING, COLE? I'M PRETTY SURE YOU PASSED.
End.

THE TRAP

THEN WE'RE DECIDED?

IT'S RISKY, COLE. VERY RISKY.

WHAT IF WE FAIL?

SIMPLE ANSWER: WE CAN'T AFFORD TO FAIL.

IT'S DO THIS OR DO NOTHING.

YOU'RE RIGHT.

SAMUKAI AND HIS SKELETONS HAVE BEEN COMING AFTER US.

IT'S TIME WE TOOK THE BATTLE TO THEM.

GREG (THE MASTERMIND) FARSHTEY -- WRITER • PAULO (THE ENFORCER) HENRIQUE -- ARTIST
LAURIE E. (THE BAIT) SMITH -- COLORIST • BRYAN (THE GO-BETWEEN) SENKA -- LETTERER
MICHAEL (THE NEGOTIATOR) PETRANEK -- ASSOCIATE EDITOR • JIM (THE PATSY) SALICRUP -- EDITOR-IN-CHIEF

OKAY, LISTEN CARE-FULLY.

HERE'S HOW WE WILL DEFEAT THE SKELETONS ONCE AND FOR ALL.

Hidden in the trees nearby, General Kruncha hears all...

SAMUKAI WILL REWARD ME FOR BRINGING HIM THIS NEWS.

THE NINJA ARE PLANNING THEIR OWN DOOM!

Later...
SAMUKAI! YOU MUST HEAR THIS!
GREAT ONE, THE NINJA ARE PLOTTING AGAINST YOU.
THEY ARE BAITING A TRAP NEAR THE KATANA RIVER. WE MUST STRIKE AT ONCE!
YOU DARE TO TELL ME WHAT WE "MUST" DO?!
MY LEGIONS ARE A HAMMER, KRUNCHA, BUT MIN IS THE HAND THA WIELDS IT.
NOW YOU WILL TELL ME EVERY DETAIL, AND I WILL DECIDE HOW BEST TO PROCEED.
MY WAGER WITH LORD GARMADON IS AS GOOD AS WON.
IS IT, SAMUKAI?
I COULD SAVE YOU MUCH GRIEF, NO DOUBT, BUT WHERE WOULD BE THE FUN IN THAT?
MY APOLOGIES, GREAT ONE.
THE NINJA PLAN TO SPREAD THE WORD IN THE VILLAGES THAT SENSEI WU WILL BE MEDITATING BY THE SHORES OF THE KATANA.
THEN THEY WILL TAKE UP POSITIONS AT FOUR PRE-ARRANGED POINTS TO AWAIT OUR COMING.

"LET THEM SET THEIR TRAP," GROWLS SAMUKAI. "WE WILL SPRING IT ON THEM."
ALL SET?
WE'VE TOLD SO MANY PEOPLE SENSEI WU WOULD BE BY THE RIVER THAT THE SENSEI HIMSELF PROBABLY BELIEVES IT BY NOW.
ALL RIGHT, GET INTO POSITION -- AND BE CAREFUL.
WHAT IS HE SO WORRIED ABOUT?
I'M ALWAYS CAREFUL... WELL, SOMETIMES... OKAY, HARDLY EVER.
LOOK AT THE FOOL, ENJOYING HIS LAST MOMENTS OF FREEDOM.
GET HIM!

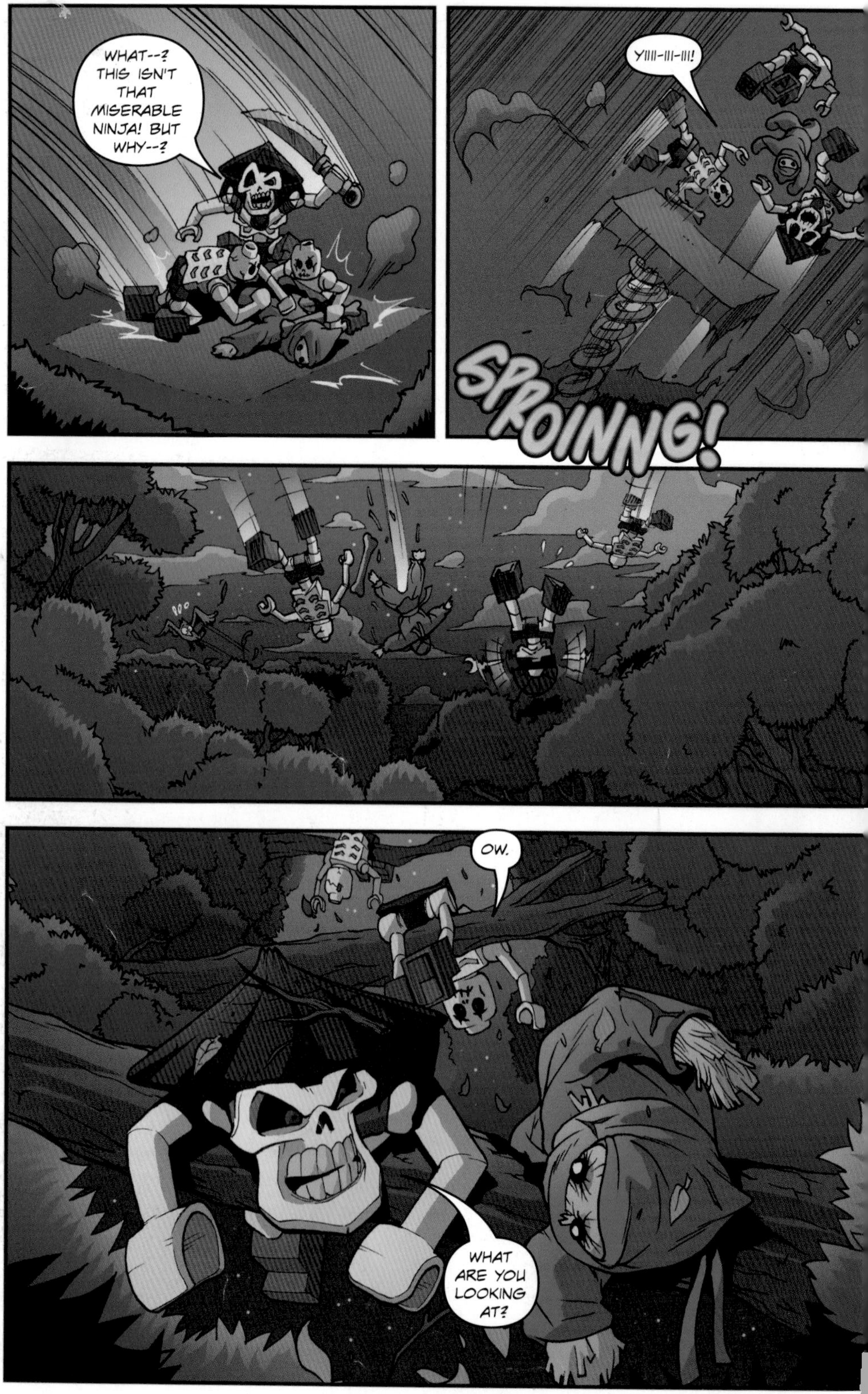

WHAT--? THIS ISN'T THAT MISERABLE NINJA! BUT WHY--?

YIIII-III-III!
SPROINNG!

OW.
WHAT ARE YOU LOOKING AT?

SEE? TOLD YOU HEY WOULD BE HERE.
WOW! SAMUKAI IS SURE TO REWARD YOU FOR THIS. HE MIGHT EVEN LET YOU SCRUB HIS THRONE!

NOW, WATCH-- I'LL SHOW YOU HOW TO DEAL WITH NINJA.

HUH?
Suddenly, unexpectedly, a previously unseen rope pulls taut...

...And quickly pulls the false ninja up, releasing a hidden surprise...
UH-OH...

SPLORCH
YUCK! WHO WOULD LEAVE A BUCKET OF GLUE UP A TREE LIKE THAT?
NUCKAL? JUST BE QUIET.

REPORT. HOW IS IT GOING SO FAR?
TWO IN THE GLUE TRAP.
THREE IN THE TREES.

FOUR FELL IN THE PIT WHILE ATTEMPTING TO DO BODILY HARM TO A STICK FIGURE THEY THOUGHT WAS ME.

AND I CAUGHT THREE WITH A DRAGON ROPE PUZZLE CAGE. BUT I DIDN'T SEE SAMUKAI. DID ANY OF YOU?
NOT ME. OLD FOUR-A IS HARD T MISS, TO

MAYBE HE CHICKENED OUT AND DIDN'T COME.
UNLIKELY. PERHAPS HE WAS SIMPLY DELAYED AND WILL FALL INTO ONE OF OUR OTHER TRAPS.

OR PERHAPS--

YOU HAVE JUST BEEN LOOKING IN THE WRONG DIRECTION.

DID YOU THINK A SKILLED COMMANDER LIKE MYSELF WOULD FALL FOR YOUR CRUDE DEVICES?
TRULY, HOW STUPID DO YOU THINK I AM?

HOW STUPID DO WE THINK HE IS?
THAT IS AN EXCELLENT QUESTION.
WELL, HE ALWAYS DID GET RIGHT TO THE POINT.
COLE, EXACTLY HOW STUPID DO WE THINK HE IS?

OH, ABOUT THIS STUPID...
NOW!
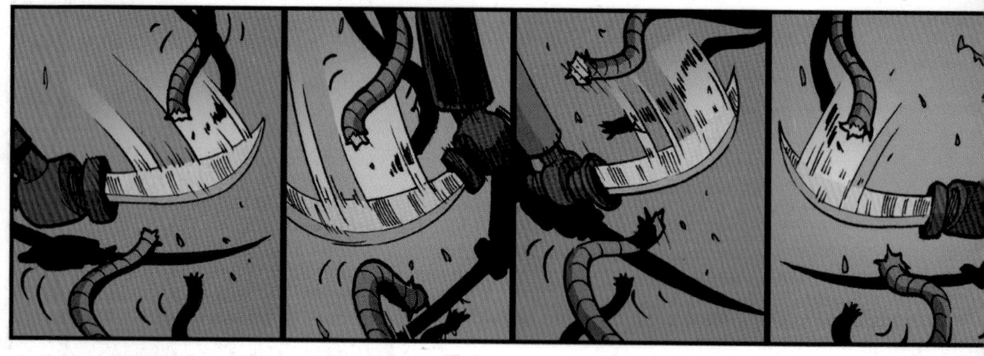

YOU DARE?!?
DON'T JUST STAND THERE, WARRIORS, CUT YOURSELVES FREE! FAST!

GOT NEWS FOR YOU--
"FAST" IS OUR SPECIALTY.

e battle
s quick.
Caught by surprise, the skeletons have no time to defend themselves.
Seemingly everywhere at once, four ninja might as well be 400.
Although some of the skeletons also know spinjitzu, they cannot match the skill of Zane and the rest.
t didn't take long for Samukai to
ee how the fight was going to end...
THE FOOLS MAY TURN MY WARRIORS INTO A BONEYARD, BUT THEY WON'T CATCH ME.

I CAN RETREAT TO THE UNDER-WORLD--

ONCE IN MY DOMAIN, I AM FREE TO PLOT MY REVENGE.

I THINK NOT.
GARMADON! HOW DID YOU--? I MEAN, WHAT IS THE MEANING OF THIS? OUT OF MY WAY!

YOU SET OUT ON A GREAT EXPEDITION TO CAPTURE FOUR NINJA.
AND NOW I SEE YOU, RETURNING ALONE, WITH YOUR LEGION NOWHERE IN SIGHT. WHATEVER COULD THAT MEAN?

A MINOR SETBACK, AT WORST.

WE MADE A WAGER, YOU AND I.

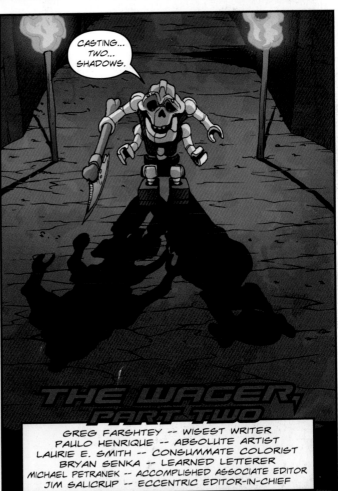

CASTING... TWO... SHADOWS.

THE WAGER, PART TWO

GREG FARSHTEY -- WISEST WRITER
PAULO HENRIQUE -- ABSOLUTE ARTIST
LAURIE E. SMITH -- CONSUMMATE COLORIST
BRYAN SENKA -- LEARNED LETTERER
MICHAEL PETRANEK -- ACCOMPLISHED ASSOCIATE EDITOR
JIM SALICRUP -- ECCENTRIC EDITOR-IN-CHIEF

DID YOU REALLY THINK YOU COULD OUTRUN YOUR DEBT TO ME, SAMUKAI?
DEBT? I OWE YOU NOTHING! IT IS YOU WHO OWE ME!

TELL ME MORE. IF YOU AMUSE ME SUFFICIENTL I MIGHT MAKE YOUR END A QUICK ONE.

GARMADON, YOU ARE A... A FOOL! DID YOU NOT SEE THE... UM.... GENIUS OF MY PLAN?
BRAKKK
WHY, OF COURSE. AFTER ALL, YOU FAILED IN SUCH CREATIVE WAYS.
SKRAKKK
NO, NO... I SEE IT ALL NOW. OF COURSE!
YOU FAILED ON PURPOSE T LURE THE NINJ INTO A FALSE SENSE OF SECURITY.

SORRY.
I HAD A FRIEND
WHO TRIED THAT.
IDN'T WORK OUT
WELL FOR HIM
EITHER, SAD
TO SAY.
KZZZAAKKKK
YOU CAN'T DO THIS TO ME! WITHOUT MY SKELETON ARMY, YOU ARE NOTHING!
I WILL STILL HAVE YOUR ARMY, BUT I WILL LEAD THEM NOW INSTEAD OF YOU. I AM SIMPLY ELIMINATING THE MIDDLE SKELETON.
GO AHEAD,
THEN. VANQUISH ME.
T'S ONLY A MATTER
F TIME BEFORE YOU
FOLLOW ME INTO
NON-EXISTENCE.
WHAT ARE YOU TALKING ABOUT? WHAT DO YOU KNOW?
FREE ME.

VERY WELL.

UNNNGH!
KKRRAASSH

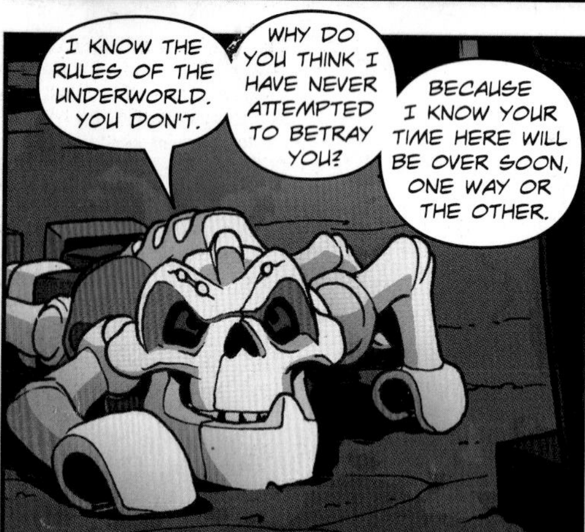
I KNOW THE RULES OF THE UNDERWORLD. YOU DON'T.
WHY DO YOU THINK I HAVE NEVER ATTEMPTED TO BETRAY YOU?
BECAUSE I KNOW YOUR TIME HERE WILL BE OVER SOON, ONE WAY OR THE OTHER.
IN YOUR SHADOW FORM, YOU CAN ONLY EXIST FOR SO LONG.
YOUR OWN WILL HAS KEPT YOU "ALIVE" ALL THESE YEARS, BUT EVEN YOU CAN ONLY RESIST THE NATURE OF THIS PLACE FOR SO LONG.

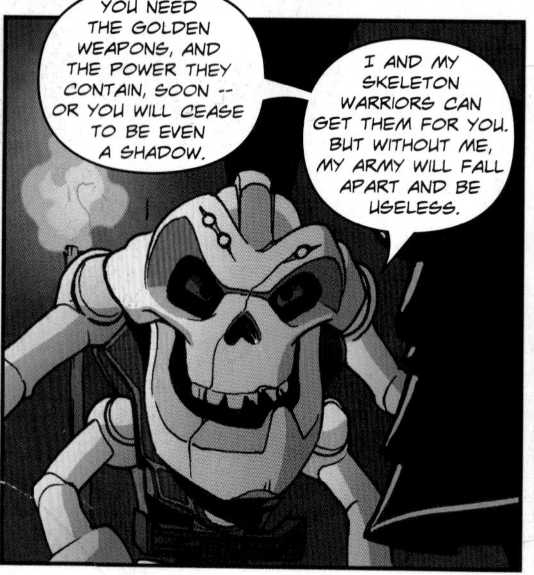
YOU NEED THE GOLDEN WEAPONS, AND THE POWER THEY CONTAIN, SOON -- OR YOU WILL CEASE TO BE EVEN A SHADOW.
I AND MY SKELETON WARRIORS CAN GET THEM FOR YOU. BUT WITHOUT ME, MY ARMY WILL FALL APART AND BE USELESS.

I MADE YOU A WAGER, AND I WON.
NOW YOU SAY I WILL BE GAMBLING MY EXISTENCE IF I TRY TO COLLECT WHAT I AM OWED--
A MOST INTERESTING PROBLEM.

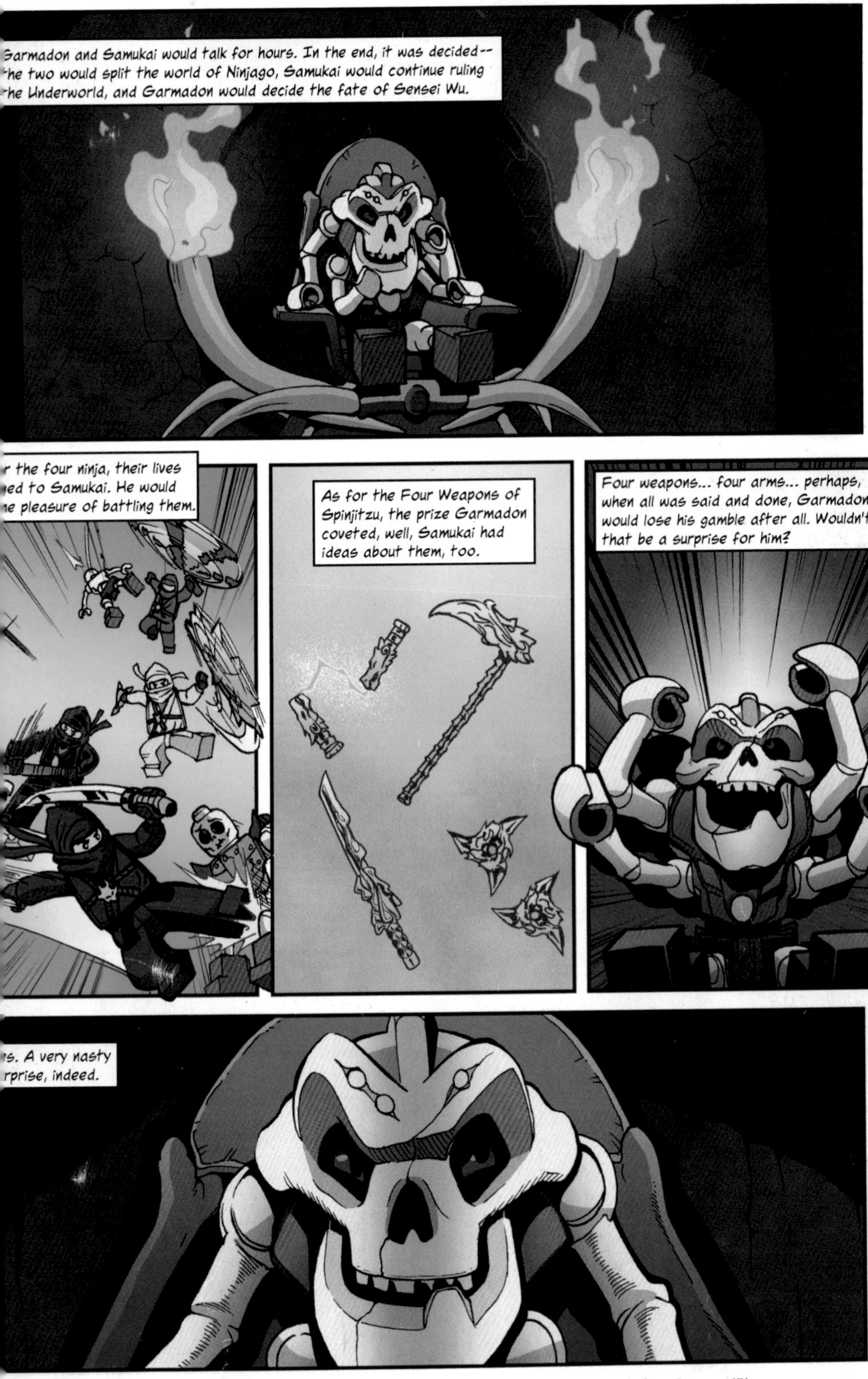

Garmadon and Samukai would talk for hours. In the end, it was decided--
the two would split the world of Ninjago, Samukai would continue ruling
the Underworld, and Garmadon would decide the fate of Sensei Wu.

r the four ninja, their lives
ed to Samukai. He would
e pleasure of battling them.

As for the Four Weapons of Spinjitzu, the prize Garmadon coveted, well, Samukai had ideas about them, too.

Four weapons... four arms... perhaps, when all was said and done, Garmadon would lose his gamble after all. Wouldn't that be a surprise for him?

s. A very nasty
rprise, indeed.

The Four Ninja Will Return in LEGO® NINJAGO #2 "Mask of the Sensei"!

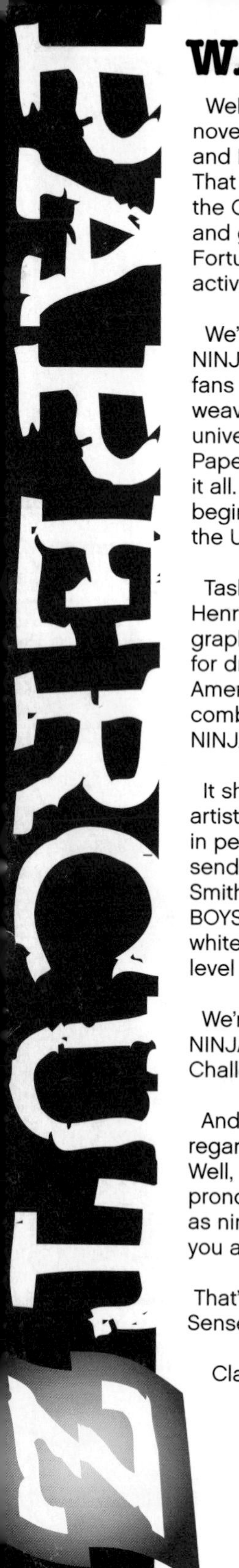

WATCH OUT FOR PAPERCUTZ

Welcome to the power-packed premiere of the LEGO® NINJAGO graphic novel series from Papercutz. I'm Jim Salicrup, the Editor-in-Chief of Papercutz and Master of Spinjitzu. Being Editor-in-Chief is like being a sensei, in a way. That would sort of make Associate Editor Michael Petranek my student in the Comics Arts. But while we may know a few things about putting comics and graphic novels together—neither one of us can claim to be a ninja! Fortunately, Jay, Cole, Zane, Kai, and Nya are here to deal with any ninja activity that may arise!

We're also lucky that the great Greg Farshtey is here to write all new NINJAGO adventures for us at Papercutz! Greg built a huge following of loyal fans with his BIONICLE® writing—which included comics and novels—by deft weaving tales set in the world of Mata-Nui! Greg was able to build an amazin universe of heroes and villains that was so detailed and fascinating, that Papercutz published two separate Guide Books to help fans fully understand it all. And now Greg Farshtey is here to be our guide to the world of Ninjago, beginning with a tale that springs from a bet made by two deadly denizens c the Underworld—Samukai and Garmadon!

Tasked with bringing Greg's script's to graphic life is none other than Paulo Henrique. Paulo had been doing a spectacular job on THE HARDY BOYS graphic novels for several years at Papercutz, and built quite a reputation for drawing in a dynamic fashion that combines the best elements of American super-hero comics with the stylized graphics of Manga. That uniqu combination made him our top choice to take on the artistic challenges of NINJAGO!

It should be noted, however, that Paulo Henrique, like most comicbook artists, creates his artwork in black and white. First drawing the comics page in pencil, and then refining his work in black ink, using pen and brush, he the sends us computer scans of his finished work. It's none other than Laurie E. Smith, who actually adds the breath-taking color-- like she did in THE HARDY BOYS. No matter how exciting we may think Paulo's artwork looks in black an white, we're always impressed by how Laurie is able to add a whole 'nother level of dazzling depth and dimension with her creative color choices!

We're proud to have assembled this awesome team of top talents for LEGO NINJAGO, and we can't wait to hear your reactions to LEGO NINJAGO #1 "The Challenge of Samukai!"

And speaking of NINJAGO, one of the questions we're asked most often regarding the Masters of Spinjitzu is exactly how is "NINJAGO" pronounced? Well, ol' Sensei Salicrup actually has the answer to that one! As a battle cry it' pronounced like it's two words—"ninja" and "go,"—otherwise it's pronounced as nin-jah-go. But if you've seen the Ninjago TV series on Cartoon Network you already knew that!

That's all for now. There's more action on the way in NINJAGO #2 "Mask of th Sensei" coming soon!

Class dismissed!

STAY IN TOUCH!

EMAIL:	salicrup@papercutz.com
WEB:	www.papercutz.com
TWITTER:	@papercutzgn
FACEBOOK:	PAPERCUTZGRAPHICNOVEI
SNAIL MAIL:	Papercutz, 160 Broadway Suite 700, East Wing New York, NY 10038